Favorite Fairy Tales

TOLD IN SPAIN

D1262214

Favorite Fairy Tales

TOLD IN SPAIN

Retold by Virginia Haviland

Illustrated by Monique Passicot

A Beech Tree Paperback Book  *New York*

First Beech Tree Edition, 1995, published by arrangement with Little, Brown and Co.

Printed in the United States of America

10 9 8 7 6 5 4 3 2 1

These stories have been adapted from the following sources:

"The Flea," from *Picture Tales from Spain* by Ruth Sawyer. (Copyright 1936 by J.B. Lippincott Company. Published by J.B. Lippincott Company.)

"The Enchanted Mule," from *The Elm-Tree Fairy Book* by Clifton Johnson. (Boston, Little, Brown and Company, 1908.) By permission of the Clifton Johnson estate.

"The Half-Chick," from *The Green Fairy Book* by Andrew Lang. (New York, Longmans, Green and Company, Inc., 1899.)

"The Carlanco," from *Spanish Fairy Tales* by Fernan Caballero. (New York, A.L. Burt Company.)

"Juan Cigarron," by Ruth Sawyer, copyright 1941 by Story Parade, Inc. Reprinted by permission of the author.

"Four Brothers Who Were Both Wise and Foolish," by Ruth Sawyer, copyright 1946 by Story Parade, Inc. Reprinted by permission of the author.

Library of Congress Cataloging-in-Publication Data

Haviland, Virginia, 1911-1988
     Favorite fairy tales told in Spain / retold by Virginia Haviland ; illustrated by Monique Passicot.
       p.   cm.
     Summary: Includes The flea, Four brothers who were both wise and foolish, The half-chick, The carlanco, Juan Cigarron, and The enchanted mule.
     ISBN 0-688-12605-7 (pbk.)
     1. Fairy tales—Spain.   [1. Fairy tales.   2. Folklore—Spain.]
I. Title.
PZ8.H295Favv 1995
398.21'0946—dc20   153 843/   94-1499
                                 CIP
                                 AC

Minor editorial and style changes have been made in the stories for these new editions.

To Ann Potter,
for her faith in my work,
— M.P.

Contents

Favorite Fairy Tales

TOLD IN SPAIN

The Flea

O NCE THERE WAS AND WAS NOT a King of Spain. He loved to laugh; he loved a good joke as well as any fellow. Best of all he loved a riddle.

One day he was being dressed by his Chamberlain. As the royal doublet was being slipped over the King's royal head, a flea jumped from the safe hiding place of the stiff lace ruff. It landed directly upon the King.

Quicker than half a wink, the King clapped his hand over the flea and began to laugh. *"Por Dios, a flea!* Who ever heard of a King of Spain having a flea? It is monstrous—it is delicious! We must not treat her lightly, this flea. You understand, My Lord Chamberlain, that having jumped on the royal person, she has now become a royal flea. Consider what we shall do with her."

But the Chamberlain was a man of little wit. He could clothe the King's body, but he could not add one ribbon or one button to the King's imagination.

"I have it!" said the King at last, exploding again into laughter. "We will pasture out this flea in a great cage large enough for a goat—an ox—an elephant. She shall be fed enormously. When she is of a proper size, I will have her killed and her skin made into a tambourine. The Infanta, my daughter, shall dance to it. We will make a fine riddle out of it. Whichever of her suitors can answer the riddle shall marry her. *There* is a royal joke worthy of a King! Eh, My Lord Chamberlain? And we will call the flea Felipa."

In his secret heart the Chamberlain thought the King quite mad, but all he answered was, "Very good, Your Majesty!" Then he went out to see that proper pasturage was provided for Felipa.

At the end of a fortnight, the flea was as large as a rat. At the end of a month, she was as large as a cat who might have eaten that rat. At the end of a second month, she was the size of a dog who might have chased that cat. At the end of three months, she was the size of a calf.

The King ordered Felipa killed. Her skin was stretched, dried, beaten until it was as soft and fine as silk. Then it was made into a tambourine, with brass clappers and ribbons—the finest tambourine in all of Spain.

The Infanta, whose name was Isabel, but who was called Belita for convenience, learned to dance with Felipa very prettily; and the King himself composed a rhyme to go with the riddle. Whenever a suitor came courting, the Infanta would dance.

When she had finished, the King would recite:

> *Belita—Felipa—they dance well together—*
> *Belita—Felipa; now answer me whether*
> *You know this Felipa—this* animalita.
> *If you answer right, then you marry Belita.*

Princes and Dukes came from Spain and Portugal, France and Italy. They were not dull-witted like the Chamberlain, and they saw through the joke. The King was riddling about the tambourine. It was made from parchment, and they thought they knew perfectly well where parchment came from.

So a Prince would answer: "A goat, Your Majesty."

And a Duke would answer: "A sheep, Your Majesty."

Each was sure that he was right.

And the Infanta would run away laughing, and the King would roar with delight and shout: "Wrong again!"

But after a while the King got tired of this sheep-and-goat business. He wanted the riddle guessed. He wanted the Infanta married. So he sent forth a command that the next suitor who failed to guess the riddle should be hanged— and short work made of it, too.

That put a stop to the Princes and Dukes. But, far up in the Castilian highlands, a shepherd heard about the riddle. He was young, but not very clever. He thought: It would be a fine thing for a shepherd to marry an Infanta. So he said to his younger brother, "Manuelito, you shall mind the sheep and goats. I will go to the King's palace."

But his mother said, "Son, you are a fool. How should you guess a riddle when you cannot read or write, and those who can have failed? Stay at home and save yourself a hanging."

But having once made up his mind, nothing would stop him—not even fear. So his mother baked him a tortilla to carry with him, gave him her blessing, and let him go.

The shepherd hadn't gone far when he was stopped by a little black ant. "Señor Pastor," she cried, "give me a ride to the King's Court in your pouch."

"Señorita Ant, you cannot ride in my pouch. There is a tortilla there which I shall have for my breakfast. Your feet are dirty from walking, and you will tramp all over it."

"See, I will dust off my feet on the grass here and promise not to step once on the tortilla."

So the shepherd put the ant into his shepherd's pouch and tramped on. Soon he encountered a black beetle, who said, "Señor Pastor, give me a ride to the King's Court in your pouch."

"Señor Beetle, you cannot ride in my pouch. There is a tortilla there which I shall presently have for my breakfast—and who wants a black beetle tramping all over his breakfast?"

"I will fasten my claws into the side of your pouch and not go near the tortilla."

So the shepherd took up the beetle and carried him along. He hadn't gone far when he came up to a little gray mouse, who cried, "Señor Pastor, give me a ride to the King's Court in your pouch."

But the shepherd shook his head. "Señor Mouse, you are too clumsy; and I don't like the flavor of your breath. It will spoil my tortilla that I intend to have for my breakfast."

"Why not eat the tortilla now, and then the breakfast will be over and done with?" The mouse said this so gently, so coaxingly, that the shepherd thought it was a splendid idea. He sat down and ate the tortilla. He gave a little crumb to Señorita Ant, a crumb to Señor Beetle, and a big crumb to Señor Mouse. Then he went on his road to the King's Court, carrying the three creatures with him in his pouch.

When he reached the King's palace, he was frightened. He sat himself down under a dark tree to wait for his courage to grow.

"What are you waiting for?" called the ant, the beetle, and the mouse all together.

"I go to answer a riddle. If I fail, I shall be hanged. That isn't so pleasant—so I'm waiting here where I can enjoy being alive for a little moment longer."

"What is the riddle?"

"I have heard that it has to do with something called Felipa that dances, whoever she may be."

"Go on, and we will help you. Hurry, hurry! It is hot in your pouch."

So the shepherd climbed the palace steps and told the guard he had come to answer the riddle.

The guard passed him on to the footman, saying, "*Pobrecito*—poor little wretch!"

The footman passed him on to the lackey, saying, "*Pobrecito!*"

The lackey passed him on to the Court Chamberlain, saying "*Pobrecito!*"

And it was the Chamberlain's business to present him to the King.

The King shook his head when he saw the shepherd's staff in the young man's hand and the shepherd's pouch hanging from his belt. He said, "A shepherd's life is better than no life at all. Better go back to your flocks."

But the shepherd was as rich in stubbornness as he was poor in learning. He insisted he must answer the riddle. So the Infanta came and danced with the tambourine, and the King laughed and said his rhyme:

Belita—Felipa—they dance well together—
Belita—Felipa; now answer me whether
You know this Felipa—this animalita.
If you answer right, then you marry Belita.

The shepherd strode over and took the tambourine from the hand of the Infanta. He felt the skin carefully, carefully. To himself he said: I know sheep, and I know goats, and this isn't either.

"Can't you guess?" whispered the black beetle from his pouch.

"No," said the shepherd.

"Let me out," said the little ant, "perhaps I can tell you what it is." So the shepherd unfastened the pouch and Señorita Ant crawled out, unseen by the Court. She crawled all over the tambourine and came back whispering, "You can't fool me. I'd know a flea anywhere, any size."

"Don't take all day," shouted the King. "Who is Felipa?"

"She's a flea," said the shepherd. Then the Court was in a flutter.

"I don't want to marry a shepherd," said the Infanta.

"You shan't," said the King.

"I'm the one to say *shan't*," said the shepherd.

"I will grant you any other favor," said the Infanta.

"I will grant you another," said the King.

"It was a long journey here, walking," said the shepherd. "I'd like a cart to ride home in."

"And two oxen to draw it," whispered the black beetle.

"And two oxen to draw it," repeated the shepherd.

"You shall have them," said the King.

"And what shall I give you?" asked the Infanta.

"Tell her you want your pouch filled with gold," whispered Señor Mouse.

"That's little enough," said the Infanta.

But while the royal groom was fetching the

cart and oxen, and the Lord of the Treasury was fetching a bag of gold, Señor Mouse was gnawing a hole in the pouch. When they came to pour in the gold, it fell through as fast as water, so that all around the feet of the shepherd it rose like a shining yellow stream.

"That's a great amount of gold," said the King at last.

"It's enough," said the shepherd. He took his cart, filled it with the gold, and drove back to the highlands of Castile. He married a shepherd's daughter, who never had to do anything but sit in a rocking chair and fan herself all day. And that's a contented life, you might say—for anyone who likes it.

Four Brothers Who Were Both Wise and Foolish

ONCE, LONG AGO, and this is the truth, there lived in Spain a farmer who had four sons: Ricardo, Roberto, Alfredo, and Bernardo.

The three older sons were wild and reckless. To plow the fields was for them a hateful task. To plant corn and wheat was a dull way to spend one's life. To milk goats was both foul-smelling and stupid.

"This is no sort of life for adventurous lads like us," said the three.

But Bernardo, the youngest, was cut from a different piece of cloth. He liked the push of the plow under his hands. He sang as he sowed the grain. And when he milked the goats, he had pleasant thoughts.

By working hard all the time—yesterday, to-day, and tomorrow—their father had at last saved one silver peso. It was not much, but it was better than nothing.

He called his sons in from the fields and said to them, "This is my entire fortune. You have worked well. Divide this among you, and go wherever your fancy leads you."

The four lads split the peso into quarter-pieces. Each put one in his pocket.

"Now we can seek our fortunes," said Ricardo.

"After that we will seek adventures," said Roberto.

"One of us must marry a King's daughter," said Alfredo.

But Bernardo shook his head. "I don't care much about doing any of those things. I'd far rather stay at home."

His brothers scoffed. They called him a fool. They called him a silly fellow, a buffoon. They said he did not know when he was well off.

So, when they took their departure, Bernardo went with them. Hay foot, straw foot, each followed his brother's heels until they came to a place where four roads crossed. Here they halted.

"Let us separate now," said Ricardo. "Let each of us follow his own road and find what fortune awaits him. At the end of a year, we will meet here. Is it agreed?"

"Agreed," said Roberto and Alfredo.

But Bernardo shook his head: "I don't care about going any farther. I'd rather go home."

But the others pulled him about, and called him a simpleton.

"I will take the road going north," said Ricardo.

"I will take the road going east," said Roberto.

"And I—the road south," said Alfredo.

That left for Bernardo the road going west. He took it with small comfort and tramped off without looking back.

On the road north, Ricardo was set upon by a band of robbers. They tied him to a donkey after they took his quarter-piece of peso and beat him for having so little wealth. Then they carried him off to their hideaway in the mountains.

In six months their leader died. Ricardo by now had shown himself so reckless and clever that they made him chief of the band.

On the road going east, Roberto traded his silver for an old gun. By turning a trick here and another there, he managed to get food to eat and bullets for his gun. He practiced shooting all day and every day, until his marksmanship became so perfect that he could clip the smallest leaf from its tree a half-mile away.

On the road south, Alfredo overtook a small man wearing enormous spectacles.

"Your glasses fit you badly," said Alfredo, "and what are you looking at?"

"Not much," said the man, "just taking a look at China. They are having a great flood there."

"Marvelous," said Alfredo.

"Tiresome," said the small man. "When you look at China, you forget Spain. When you look inside a house in Persia, you forget there is a cozy little house waiting for you in Andalusia. I have grown rich seeing too much. Now I think I will go home and look no farther than the walls around my patio. You can have the spectacles for whatever you happen to have in your pocket."

"Agreed," said Alfredo.

And he gave the small man his quarter-piece of peso.

Bernardo, the youngest brother, wandered a day and a night along his road and found nothing. He was about to turn back when he came across a coppersmith's shop.

All that second day he watched the coppersmith mending kettles, fitting copper bands about great casks, making pots and ladles and all sorts of useful things.

"If I can't be a farmer," he thought, "I will become a coppersmith." So he gave the fellow his quarter-piece to learn the trade.

At the end of the year, the four brothers met at the crossroads.

"I have become a robber chief. Anything in the world that I like, I can take for my own," said Ricardo.

"I have become the greatest marksman in Spain," said Roberto, showing off his fowling piece. "Show me the smallest object at the far-thest distance, and I can hit it."

Alfredo put on his spectacles. "I can see the Emperor of China sitting down to tea in his garden and a fly that is crawling on his nose."

Bernardo hung his head. He could not look his fine brothers in the eye.

"Come, speak up, stupid one," said the others. "What have you to show for your year?"

"Nothing worth talking about. I am just a poor coppersmith. I can mend a pot or a kettle—that is all. Now let us go home."

The others laughed till their sides ached, calling him a goose—a simpleton—a buffoon—the worst one in all of Spain. "If we let you go home now, you would remain a simpleton all your life. You shall come with us on our adventure."

Alfredo looked all around the world to see in what direction adventure might lie. "Oh-oh!" he said at last, and pointed to the east. "Yonder lies the sea. On the sea lies an island. On the island sleeps a captive Princess, guarded night and day by a giant sea serpent."

"We will rescue her!" shouted Ricardo.

"Agreed!" shouted Roberto and Alfredo.

Bernardo shook his head. "I don't care much about sea serpents, or rescuing a Princess. I'd rather go home."

But the others pulled him along. And before he knew it, they were looking across the sea. They fitted up a small vessel and set sail for the island. How many days they sailed does not matter. They reached there in the dark of dawn.

Alfredo put on his spectacles and looked. "The serpent sleeps," said he. "But he is coiled around the Princess to the height of the tower."

"Does the Princess sleep?" asked Bernardo.

"Of course she sleeps. What has that to do with it?" Alfredo was scornful.

"A sleeping Princess is not apt to scream. A screaming Princess could waken a sea serpent. Let us have our coffee first."

For once the others agreed. They had their coffee. Then Ricardo was put softly ashore.

"Watch me," he whispered. "Now I will steal the Princess, for that is my profession."

Everything went well until the last moment. Then Ricardo caught his foot on the serpent's tail. The serpent woke and gave a great roar. That woke the Princess, and she screamed. That set Ricardo running hot for the beach. He swam, and the serpent swam. Ricardo boarded the ship and set down the Princess. The serpent came close, very close.

"Now," said Roberto, "I will shoot the serpent, for that is my profession."

Shoot him he did, clean through the middle. But the serpent gave three dying lashes with the end of his tail. *Flip-flap-flop!* It cut the ship

nearly in two. The three brothers and the Princess were terrified, for drowning looked very near.

"There is nothing to be scared of," said Bernardo. "Mending is my profession." He proceeded to get his tools and some long strips of copper, and he welded the two parts of the ship together until she was as good as new. "Safe and snug," said he.

They lifted anchor, and sailed to the country where the Princess's father was King. I cannot tell you if it was Greece or Persia or Asia. All I know is that the ship got there.

The King was enormously pleased to have his daughter rescued. He had been too busy with affairs of state to do it himself. And he was more than willing to reward the one who had done it. He would do it very handsomely—not only with the Princess herself, but with a large sack of gold as well.

"I rescued her," said Alfredo. And when the others looked surprised, he added, "Had I not put on my spectacles and discovered her, she would still be on the island."

"I rescued her," said Ricardo. "Didn't I steal her from the middle of the serpent's coils?"

"And stepped on his tail and woke him," reminded Roberto. "Had I not shot the serpent, where would we all be? Dead!"

The King listened solemnly. Then he pointed a finger at Bernardo: "*You*—what did you do?"

"Nothing much," said Bernardo. "When the serpent cut the ship in two, I mended it."

"Then *you* rescued the Princess." The King said it with such kingly authority that no one dared dispute him. "You shall marry the Princess."

Bernardo shook his head. "I don't care much about being the husband of a Princess," he said. "I would rather go home."

"Come, come!" said the King.

"Come, come!" said the brothers.

"Come," said the Princess. "I'll go with you. I've always wanted to milk a goat.

So they all separated. Ricardo took the road north and went back to his robber band. Roberto took his gun and went east. Alfredo put on his spectacles and stepped high into the south. But Bernardo and the Princess went west, singing all the way home.

The Half-Chick

ONCE UPON A TIME there was a hand-some black Spanish hen who had a large brood of chickens. They were all fine, plump little birds except the youngest, who was quite unlike his brothers and sisters. Indeed, he was such a queer-looking creature that when he first cracked his shell, his mother could scarcely believe her eyes.

He was so different from the twelve downy little chicks who nestled under her wings! This one looked just as if he had been cut in two. He had only one leg, and one wing, and one eye, and he had half a head and half a beak. His mother shook her head sadly as she looked at him and said, "My youngest-born is only a half-chick. He can never grow up to be a tall handsome cock like his brothers. They will go out into the world and rule over poultry yards of their own, but this poor little fellow will always have to stay at home with his mother." She called him *Medio Pollito*, which is Spanish for Half-Chick.

Now, though Medio Pollito was such an odd, helpless-looking little thing, his mother soon found that he was not at all willing to remain at home under her wing. Indeed, he was as unlike his brothers and sisters in disposition as he was in appearance. They were good, obedient chickens, and when the old hen clucked after them, they chirped and ran back to her side. But Medio Pollito had a roving spirit, in spite of his one leg. When his mother called to him to return to the coop, he pretended that he could not hear because he had only one ear.

When she took the whole family out for a walk in the fields, Medio Pollito would hop away by himself and hide among the corn. Many an anxious minute his brothers and sisters spent looking for him, while his mother ran to and fro cackling in fear and dismay.

As Medio Pollito grew older, he became more self-willed and disobedient. His manner to his mother was often rude and his behavior to the other chickens disagreeable.

One day he was away in the fields for an excursion longer than usual. On his return he strutted up to his mother with the peculiar little hop and kick that was his way of walking.

Cocking his one eye at her in a bold way, he said, "Mother, I am tired of this life in a dull farmyard, with nothing but a dreary cornfield to look at. I'm off to Madrid to see the King."

"To Madrid, Medio Pollito!" exclaimed his mother. "Why, you silly chick, that would be a long journey for a grown-up cock. A poor little thing like you would be tired out before you had gone half the distance. No, no, stay at home with your mother. Some day, when you are bigger, we will go on a little journey together."

But Medio Pollito had made up his mind. He would not listen to his mother's advice nor to the prayers and entreaties of his brothers and sisters.

"What is the use of our all crowding each other in this poky little place?" said Medio Pollito. "When I have a fine courtyard of my own at the King's palace, I shall perhaps ask some of you to come and pay me a short visit."

Scarcely waiting to say good-bye to his family, away he stumped down the highroad that led to Madrid.

"Be sure that you are kind and polite to everyone you meet," called his mother, running after him. But he was in such a hurry to be off that he did not wait to answer her or even to look back.

A little later in the day, as he was taking a shortcut through a field, he passed a stream. Now, the stream was all choked up and overgrown with weeds and water plants, so its waters could not flow freely.

"O Medio Pollito!" it cried, as the half-chick hopped along its banks. "Do come and help me by clearing away these weeds."

"Help you, indeed!" exclaimed Medio Pollito, tossing his head and shaking the few feathers in his tail. "Do you think I have nothing to do but to waste my time on such trifles? Help yourself, and don't trouble busy travelers. I am off to

Madrid to see the King." And *hoppity-kick,* *hoppity-kick,* away stumped Medio Pollito.

A little later he came to a fire that had been left by some gypsies in a wood. It was burning very low and would soon be out.

"O Medio Pollito!" cried the fire in a weak, wavering voice as the half-chick approached. "In a few minutes I shall go out unless you put some sticks upon me. Do help me, or I shall die!"

"Help you, indeed!" answered Medio Pollito. "I have other things to do. Gather sticks for yourself, and don't trouble me. I am off to Madrid to see the King." And *hoppity-kick,* *hoppity-kick,* away stumped Medio Pollito.

The next morning, as he was getting near Madrid, he passed a large chestnut tree in whose branches the wind was caught and entangled.

"O Medio Pollito!" called the wind. "Do hop up here and help me to get free of these branches.

I cannot pull away, and it is so uncomfortable!"

"It is your own fault for stopping there," answered Medio Pollito. "I can't waste all my morning here helping you. Just shake yourself free, and don't hinder me. I am off to Madrid to see the King." And *hoppity-kick, hoppity-kick,* away stumped Medio Pollito in great glee, for the towers and roofs of Madrid were now in sight.

When he entered the town, he saw before him a splendid house with soldiers standing before its gates. This he knew must be the King's palace. He determined to hop up to the front gate and wait until the King came out. But, as he hopped past the back windows, the King's cook saw him.

"Here is the very thing I need," he exclaimed, "for the King has just sent a message that he must have chicken broth for his dinner!" Opening the window, the cook stretched forth his arm, caught Medio Pollito, and popped him into the broth pot that was standing near the fire. Oh, how wet and clammy the water felt as it went over Medio Pollito's head! It made his feathers cling to him.

"O Water, Water!" he cried in his despair. "Do have pity and cease wetting me like this!"

"Ah, Medio Pollito!" replied the water. "You would not help me when I was a little stream away in the fields. Now you must be punished."

Then the fire began to burn. It scalded Medio Pollito and made him dance and hop from one side of the pot to the other to get away from the heat.

He cried out in pain, "Fire, Fire! Do not scorch me like this! You can't think how it hurts!"

"Ah, Medio Pollito!" answered the fire. "You would not help me when I was dying away in the wood. You are being punished."

At last, just when the pain was so great that Medio Pollito thought he must die, the cook lifted up the lid of the pot to see if the broth was ready for the King's dinner.

"Look here!" he cried in horror. "This chicken is quite useless. It is burned to a cinder. I can't send this up to the royal table." Opening the window, the cook threw Medio Pollito out into the street. The wind now caught the half-chick and whirled him through the air so quickly that Medio Pollito could scarcely breathe. His heart beat against his side till he thought it would break.

"O Wind!" he gasped at last. "If you hurry me along like this, you will kill me. Do let me rest a moment, or—"

The half-chick was so breathless that he could not finish his sentence.

"Ah, Medio Pollito!" replied the wind. "When I was caught in the branches of the chestnut tree you would not help me. Now you are punished." And the wind swirled Medio Pollito over the

roofs of the houses until they came to the highest church in town. There the wind left Medio Pollito fastened to the top of the steeple.

And there stands Medio Pollito to this day. If you go to Madrid and walk through the streets till you come to the highest church, you will see Medio Pollito perched on his one leg on the steeple. His one wing droops at his side, and out of his one eye he gazes sadly over the town.

The Carlanco

ONCE UPON A TIME IN SPAIN, there was a goat who was a very good mother and housekeeper. She had three well-behaved little kids, which she had brought up most carefully.

One day when the mother was up on the mountain gathering wood, she saw a wasp that was near to drowning in a stream. With quick wit, she held out a branch. The wasp managed to get hold of it, and then the goat was able to pull her to land.

"Heaven will reward you!" said the wasp. "You have done me an act of great mercy. If ever you have any need of me, you must go to that old wall, where I live as Abbess of our convent of wasps. I have many little cells there which are in ruins, as we are very poor. But inquire for the Abbess, and I will come at once to help you. I will do for you all that I can. *Adiós*—Farewell."

After saying this, the wasp flew away, singing her morning prayers.

A few days later, early in the morning, the goat said to her little ones, "I am going to the mountain for a bundle of wood. You must shut yourselves in and bar up the door. Be very careful not to open to anyone, because that wicked ogre, the Carlanco, is roving about. Do not open the door until I say to you:

Open the door, my children three.
I am your mother, so open for me!

The goat went away, and the little kids, who were very dutiful, did exactly what she had told them to do. Soon they heard someone calling at the door in a great rough voice:

Open the door,
The Carlanco is here!

The little kids had barred the door heavily, so they shouted from within:

Open it yourself, strong one!

The Carlanco tried to push the door open, but he could not. Finally he went away in a rage, promising the kids that he would get them yet.

Later the mother goat returned with her load of wood and called in to her three little kids:

Open the door, my children three.
I am your mother, so open for me!

The next day the Carlanco hid nearby. When the mother goat returned, he listened to what she said to the little kids—the same words she had used the day before.

The following morning the Carlanco hid again. When the mother departed, and he thought she had gone far enough away, he went to the door. Imitating her voice, he said:

Open the door, my children three.
I am your mother, so open for me!

The little kids this time believed that it was their mother calling to them. They went to the door and opened it. Now they saw that it was the horrible Carlanco himself! Off they scampered with all their might up the ladder, which they pulled up after them. Thus they got onto the roof where the Carlanco could not reach them.

The monster was in a passion at this. He could see them, but he could not reach them. Finally,

he closed the door and began raging about the house, snorting so fiercely that the poor little kids shivered with fright.

Presently their mother came home with her load of wood. She called to her kids to open the door, but they cried down to her from the roof that the Carlanco was in the house.

When the goat heard this she flung down her wood and, with the speed of lightning, flew to the convent of wasps and knocked at their door.

"Who is it?" inquired the doorkeeper.

"Mother, I am a little goat, at your service."

"A goat here, in this convent of devout wasps? Go off! I have no alms to give. Go your way, and Heaven protect you," said the doorkeeper.

"Call the Abbess to come quickly," said the goat. "If not, I will go for the bee-hunting bird whom I saw near here."

The doorkeeper was frightened at this, so she hastened to call the Abbess. To the Abbess wasp, the goat told the dreadful thing that had happened.

"Be of good heart, Mother Goat," said she. "I will help you and your kids. Let us hasten to your house."

When they arrived, the wasp crept into the house through the keyhole. She began to sting the Carlanco, now in the eyes, now on the nose, so that he was quite bewildered. He finally opened the door and ran off like a whirlwind.

Juan Cigarron

ONCE THERE WAS and was not a poor couple who had many children. The eldest was a clever rascal, always plaguing the younger ones, always turning a trick to benefit himself.

At last, when the thirteenth child was born, the father said to the eldest, "Juan Cigarron, you are a clever rascal. Go and seek your fortune. There is no longer enough in the house to eat."

So, out into God's world went Juan Cigarron. As he followed this road and that, he said to himself: I am such a good rascal, I will make a better wizard.

Juan Cigarron went on to serve as an apprentice to all the wizards in Spain until he knew how to beat them all at their game. He fooled the world to perfection. Everybody believed in him, because everybody wanted to believe in him. So he became famous.

It happened one day in the King's palace that all the silver plate disappeared. One day it was there and the King was eating from it, just as he had eaten from it every day. The next day the silver was gone—plates, goblets, trenchers and tankards—as if the earth had swallowed them.

"Send for Juan Cigarron," said the King. "I have heard that he is the greatest wizard in Spain. I believe that he may be the greatest *rascal*. We shall try him."

So a messenger was sent and Juan Cigarron was brought to the palace, straight to the hall where the King sat eating from a common clay dish.

"The royal silver is gone—stolen. You are to find it, and learn who stole it," said the King. "But you shall make your discovery while locked in the deepest dungeon in the palace. Being a great wizard, you can do your work there as well as anywhere else. If you should turn out to be a cheating rascal, instead of a wizard, we will have you there—safe, hide and hair—to hang, as a fine example. Three days now you shall have to find the royal silver."

The guards led Juan Cigarron to the dungeon. They fastened an iron ball and chain to his feet. They locked him in with a key as large as his leg bone. They left him alone all day that he might better practice his magic, and all day his heart grew heavier.

I am well caught—thought Juan Cigarron to himself—there never was a wizard who died comfortably in his bed. Already, I feel a rope about my throat. Ah me!

At the end of the day, one of the King's pages came to bring him food. In despair Juan Cigarron watched the jailer unlock the door for him to enter. He watched the page boy place the food on the bench before him, and watched him turn away. All the time he was thinking: Three days of life granted me—no more, no less—and already one is gone. As the jailer unlocked the door for the page to go out again, Juan Cigarron groaned:

Ay, by San Bruno, this is no fun;
Of the three—there goes one!

Hearing these words, the page took to his heels and ran as if the devil himself were after him. Finding the King's two other pages waiting for him in a corner of the palace wall, he told them quickly what Juan Cigarron had said.

"Not a doubt of it. He is the greatest wizard on earth. He knows we three have stolen the silver and buried it in the graveyard. We are undone. Let us go to him and confess."

"Never," said one of the others. "You are a weakling. Your ears did not hear right. Tomorrow I will carry his supper to him, and then we shall see."

At the end of the second day, Juan Cigarron's heart had become as heavy as the irons on his feet.

With agony he watched the second page enter his dungeon, leave food, and depart. He groaned:

Now, by San José, honest and true,
Of the three—I've counted two.

If one devil had been at the heels of the first

page, a score were hounding the second. "He knows—he knows!" he screamed to the two boys waiting for him. "We are lost."

"Not yet," said the third and oldest page. "I myself will carry his supper tomorrow night. I shall not run from the cell. I shall stand beside him and mark his words with care."

At the end of the third day, Juan Cigarron could feel a rope as if tied tightly about his neck. He could not eat his supper for choking. Looking up from his bench and seeing the third page still standing at his elbow, he thought: Here is a lad who feels pity for me. And aloud he said:

Good San Andrés, counsel me.
They've come and gone—all three!

The page threw himself at the jailed feet of Juan Cigarron. He groveled there, shaking with fear.

"Master Wizard, pity us! Have compassion!

Do not tell the King that it is his three pages who have stolen the silver. We will have our necks wrung tomorrow like so many cockerels if you do. Spare us and we will tell you where it lies buried. And never, never will we steal again."

With great dignity Juan Cigarron rose to his feet. "Do you not know that young rascals have a way of turning into old rascals? How do I know that by saving you now, I shall not be freeing you to commit more sins later? Enough groveling, now; I will pardon you this time. But you must swear by all the saints never to steal again—not so much as an *ochavito*. Tomorrow, when I appear before the King, you must in secret bring the silver, every last piece of it."

So on the morrow Juan Cigarron was not hanged. He told the King where the silver plate would be found. And there it was, sure enough. The King was more than pleased. He embraced

Juan Cigarron and kissed him on both cheeks.

"I did you a great wrong, and I shall make it up to you. From now on you shall be, not *a* wizard to all the world, but my own Royal Wizard. You shall live with me always, in the palace, where you will be handy to turn a magic trick when the occasion arises. You are great—stupendous— more magnificent than all the wizards in the whole wide world!" He hugged Juan Cigarron again.

So Juan Cigarron lived in the palace, eating with the King, sleeping in a room next to his, and going where the King went.

But Juan grew thinner and paler and unhappier every day. "What shall I do when the next trial comes! Ah me!" groaned Juan Cigarron, as each new hour in the day struck.

At last there came an evening when the King happened to be walking alone in his garden. He was smoking, and thinking that it was time Juan

Cigarron should have his wits and his magic put to the test again. Thinking he would play a clever trick on him, the King took his cigar from his mouth and pulled his wallet from his pocket. Into the wallet he stuffed the cigar and put them both into his pocket. Next he sent a page to bring the wizard.

When Juan Cigarron stood before him, the King asked, "What did I have in my mind that I took out of my mouth and put for safekeeping in my wallet?" He meant that he had been thinking of Cigarron, his wizard; he had been smoking *cigarron* and had put *cigarron* in his pocket.

Juan Cigarron was filled with terror. Here was doom descending upon him. Hardly knowing that he spoke, he muttered, more to himself than to the King:

What a fool is man to pretend—
Poor Juan Cigarron has met a bad end!

How the King laughed! He clapped his hand to his pocket, drew out his wallet and showed the cigar snuffed out and quite dead. Casting it from him, he embraced Juan Cigarron and said, "That was as clever an answer as ever I heard. For that, I will grant any wish you wish to make."

"Any wish?" asked Juan Cigarron.

"Any wish," confirmed the King.

"Then I wish to end my days as a wizard tonight—and begin them tomorrow as a simple man."

The Enchanted Mule

ONCE UPON A TIME there lived in Spain a poor man named Pedro whose business it was to take care of horses at an inn. Pedro was so very poor that he had to go about in rags.

One day to the inn there came an archbishop riding on a mule that was richly outfitted with the finest harness and a scarlet saddlecloth.

71

Several attendants followed on foot and helped the archbishop dismount from his elegantly decked steed.

The archbishop turned to Pedro and said, "Feed and take care of my mule for the night. In the morning I shall continue my journey."

Pedro led the mule into the stable. He removed the splendid saddle and bridle, gave the mule the very best stall, and fed it all the hay and oats it would eat.

Next morning Pedro fed the mule again. He curried it and dressed it in its gay trappings. "Ah," said he, "look at this rich attire the mule displays, while I wear rags. And look at his stout sides. He lives a comfortable life, with always the best of everything. My life, on the contrary, is full of hardship. I have only a hovel for a dwelling. And even were it a mansion I could find small pleasure in it, for when I am at home

my wife scolds me constantly. Indeed—I would gladly change places with this mule!"

Pedro leaned against a manger and laughed loud and long at this fanciful idea.

The mule looked around at him and began to speak. "What ho!" it exclaimed. "You would change places with *me*, would you? You must remember that my master is fat and heavy. A weary load, I often find him."

"But," said Pedro, "consider the good care you get every day."

"Well," replied the mule, "even so, I would like a little freedom. I would sooner be you than myself. Yes, if it is true that you would like to change places with me, just take hold of my ears and you shall become the archbishop's mule."

"That will suit me exactly," said Pedro. "Better to be a well-fed mule than a half-starved groom with a scolding wife."

Pedro grasped the mule's ears and immediately was transformed into a mule. "Now," he said, "for once I shall eat all I want. Here, boy, give me more hay and oats."

The former mule, however, was now so pleased with his human form and his escape from harness that he paid no attention to Pedro's words. At once he made his way out of the stable to stroll about in freedom.

Pedro knew that if he was now going off on a long journey with the archbishop, he ought to say good-bye to his wife and his old mother. He started to go home, but found he was tied to his stall. He pulled hard at his halter but could not get free. I'll wait till the archbishop comes for me, he thought. Then, as soon as I am led out of the stable, I will break away and run home. Pedro now began to fear that he might have made a mistake in becoming a mule.

The archbishop soon appeared and called for his mule. Since the groom could not be found, some of his own men went into the stable and returned with Pedro the mule. To their great surprise, as they were tightening the saddle, Pedro bolted away. Down the road he galloped, as fast as he could go, in the direction of his house. The archbishop thought his mule had gone mad. His servants ran down the road shouting, "Stop the beast! Stop it!" And everyone along the way joined in the wild chase.

Pedro kept running till he reached his house. There his mother sat at the door, spinning. Being deaf, she did not hear the commotion of clattering hoofs and yelling people. Pedro came close and tried to take her hand. He wanted to ask her to bless him before he went away with the archbishop. But he found he could no longer speak the language of humans. His harsh braying and his attempt to grasp his mother's hand terrified the old woman.

She sprang to her feet and hit him with her distaff, crying: "Get away, you horrid mule!"

A moment later Pedro's wife appeared in the doorway and threw a basin of water over him.

The crowd stood looking on, until some of the archbishop's servants at last seized Pedro. They tried to lead him back to the stable, but he would not go. He stood up on his hind legs. He lay down and rolled in the dirt till his handsome saddlecloth was no longer a bright scarlet. Suddenly rising, he rushed into the cottage and tried to sit on his old chair.

Pedro's mother and wife fled from the house, but the crowd entered. They whacked and thwacked Pedro so brutally that finally he was glad to give up and return to the inn. When he had been cleaned and decked again in his finery, he allowed the archbishop to mount him so they could start on their journey.

They had not gone far when the archbishop exclaimed: "Goodness! This mule rolls like a camel."

It was true. Pedro, not used to walking on four legs, did not know how to work them. He failed to move his front and rear legs together properly, and thus caused the archbishop great discomfort. Being very fat, the man pitched about in the saddle like a ship in a heavy sea. At length, afraid he would fall off, he seized the pommel with both hands and stood up in the stirrups.

At this point they were riding through a village. The people, seeing him standing this way, thought he was about to deliver a sermon. So they bared their heads and knelt to receive his blessing.

Pedro, who knew well enough what was troubling the archbishop, laughed to himself inwardly. He laughed so hard that he began to cough. The faithful people, with their heads bent, could not see the archbishop's face and supposed that the coughing came from him, as a natural clearing of his throat.

The archbishop now was truly frightened. He gave a cry of alarm.

Pedro was perplexed. Not knowing what else to do, he sat down on his hind quarters. The archbishop, of course, slid off and lay on his back on the ground. More alarmed than ever at what he had done, Pedro now quickly rose. But this only made matters worse. The archbishop first landed on his head and then went rolling in the dust.

Angry now, the archbishop scrambled to his feet. He examined his mule, but could see nothing unusual.

Pedro was truly sorry to have caused his good master so much pain and trouble. He turned toward the archbishop and went down on his

forelegs, to show by kneeling that he begged pardon. However, this only scared the villagers so that they hid behind the archbishop. The archbishop was as much afraid as they were, too. Had they not held him by his robes, he would have run away.

"See," at last cried one of the people, "the mule repents for what he has done and asks to be pardoned!"

The archbishop was not so sure about this. He backed slowly away from the strangely behaving animal. Pedro saw that he did not need to kneel any longer. He got up and stood quietly, hoping to calm his master. This worked. After watching him for some minutes, the archbishop knew that the mule meant him no harm. He found the courage to remount.

Pedro now aimed to help his master make up for the time he had lost, so he set off at a quick pace. This made the archbishop so unsteady again in the saddle that he could barely keep from falling off.

The archbishop's servants tried to keep up with him, but, as they were on foot, Pedro's rapid strides left them behind. Not until they were within sight of the city, and Pedro had slowed his pace for a time, did they catch up. The archbishop now had an attendant hold a rein on each side, and he himself held onto a shoulder of each man so that the mule should not run off again.

At the city gate, a group of priests came forth to welcome the archbishop. The leader was carrying a large silver cross. At sight of the cross, Pedro remembered his mother's teachings. He dropped to his knees before the sacred emblem and bowed his head to the ground. This he did so suddenly that the archbishop nearly flew out of the saddle. His hands, which had been on the shoulders of his servants, made a wild grasp and caught them by the hair. In their fright, they struck out right and left—and with their blows nearly stunned the archbishop.

Pedro was angry to see them treating the old archbishop in this way. To punish the servants, he got up again with the archbishop clinging to his neck. The servants fled, but Pedro ran after them, opening his mouth to bite and shake them. The servants hid among the priests, and all of them hurried into a small chapel nearby.

"Our archbishop must have exchanged mules with a demon," said the priest with the silver cross.

"But what has become of the archbishop?" asked another. "We must help him."

Carefully, they opened the chapel door. There on the highway they saw the archbishop sitting where he had fallen off the mule. He was faint with fright and quite without power to rise.

Pedro at the same time was dashing about among the crowd that had come out from the city to see what was going on. Hither and thither he galloped, knocking down many of them. Finally, he set off at his fastest speed along the road home. He did not stop running until he reached the inn where he had been a groom. Here the innkeeper hastened to tie him securely.

Pedro had time now to think about his mistake. "Ah," he mused, "I would gladly take any punishment, if only I could have my former shape again. If my wife had been right all the times she called me a donkey, I should have made a good mule. But it has been far otherwise."

Just then the groom with whom Pedro had changed places came into the stable, looking very unhappy. When he saw the archbishop's mule, he went to it and asked: "Pedro, how do you like being a mule?"

"Well," replied Pedro, who now again had the power of speech, "I enjoyed carrying the archbishop as much as he enjoyed being carried. But I am not accustomed to this sort of life, and I wish I were out of it."

"If that be the case," the groom responded, "hold down your head and we will change back to our old selves. The truth is, I never could live in the same house with your wife. By my faith, I would rather bear my master's saddle till I drop in my tracks than listen to your wife's tongue from morning till night for a single day."

"But her ways seem not so bad to one who is used to them," said Pedro, "and I am willing—"

"Hurry," interrupted the groom. "I hear her knocking at the door. Down with your head!" And the groom grasped the mule's ears.

In a twinkling they changed places. Pedro turned to meet his wife, who had some sharp things to say. But he answered so gently that her anger softened.

Indeed, remembering what he had suffered as a mule, Pedro never again spoke crossly when his wife scolded. This made her far less ready with a sharp tongue, and their home life became happier.

On the morning after the mule had returned, the innkeeper decided to learn what had happened to the archbishop. He found the archbishop unwilling to ride the creature ever again and ready to sell it for whatever the innkeeper would give.

The innkeeper bought the mule for a very small sum, and Pedro became its groom. He treated it with special friendliness and sometimes talked to it. In response, the mule looked at Pedro so brightly that Pedro knew it understood him. It never answered, but Pedro was sure this was because it was content in being what it was, and wanted no more of changing shapes.

About This Series

IN RECENT DECADES, folk tales and fairy tales from all corners of the earth have been made available in a variety of handsome collections and in lavishly illustrated picture books. But in the 1950s, such a rich selection was not yet available. The classic fairy and folk tales were most often found in cumbersome books with small print and few illustrations. Helen Jones, then children's book editor at Little, Brown and Company, accepted a proposal from a Boston librarian for an ambitious series with a simple goal — to put an international selection of stories into the hands of children. The tales would be published in slim volumes, with wide margins and ample leading, and illustrated by a cast of contemporary artists. The result was a unique series of books intended for children to read by themselves — the Favorite Fairy Tales series. Available only in hardcover for many years, the books have now been reissued in paperbacks that feature new illustrations and covers.

The series embraces the stories of sixteen different

countries: France, England, Germany, India, Ireland, Sweden, Poland, Russia, Spain, Czechoslovakia, Scotland, Greece, Japan, Denmark, Italy, and Norway. Some of these stories may seem violent or fantastical to our modern sensibilities, yet they often reflect the deepest yearnings and imaginings of the human mind and heart.

Virginia Haviland traveled abroad frequently and was able to draw upon librarians, storytellers, and writers in countries as far away as Japan to help make her selections. But she was also an avid researcher with a keen interest in rare books, and most of the stories she included in the series were found through a diligent search of old collections. Ms. Haviland was associated with the Boston Public Library for nearly thirty years — as a children's and branch librarian, and eventually as Readers Advisor to Children. She reviewed for *The Horn Book Magazine* for almost thirty years and in 1963 was named Head of the Children's Book Section of the Library of Congress. Ms. Haviland remained with the Library of Congress for nearly twenty years and wrote and lectured about children's literature throughout her career. She died in 1988.